TO EVERYONE WHO LOVES AND
SUPPORTS MY VIDEOS, I HOPE YOU
ENJOY THIS AS MUCH AS I DO.

USERNAME: EVIE

EVIE

JOE SUGG

HODDER &
STOUGHTON

First published in Great Britain in 2015 by
Hodder & Stoughton
An Hachette UK company

4

Copyright © Joe Sugg 2015
With thanks to Matt Whyman
Artwork by Amrit Birdi
Colourist: Joaquin Pereyra
Letterist: Mindy Lopkin

CIP catalogue record for this title is available from the British Library
Hardback ISBN 9781473619135
Trade paperback ISBN 9781473619159
Ebook ISBN 9781473619128

Printed and bound in Italy by Graphicom S.r.l.
Hodder & Stoughton policy is to use papers that are natural, renewable and recyclable products and made from wood grown in sustainable forests. The logging and manufacturing processes are expected to conform to the environmental regulations of the country of origin.
Carmelite House
50 Victoria Embankment
London EC4Y 0DZ

www.hodder.co.uk

HELLO THERE

MY NAME IS JOE SUGG, OTHERWISE KNOWN AS THATCHERJOE ON YOUTUBE.

FIRST OFF, I'D JUST LIKE TO SAY A MASSIVE THANK YOU FOR CHOOSING TO BUY MY FIRST EVER GRAPHIC NOVEL — MY FIRST EVER BOOK, IN FACT! I AM SO FLIPPIN' PLEASED WITH IT AND I HOPE YOU WILL BE TOO.

YOU MIGHT BE WONDERING WHERE THE INSPIRATION CAME FROM TO CREATE A GRAPHIC NOVEL. WELL, IT GOES RIGHT BACK TO GROWING UP OBSESSED WITH COMICS LIKE *THE BEANO* AND *THE DANDY* — I STILL HAVE ALL MY OLD COPIES CLOGGING UP THE ATTIC BACK HOME... SORRY, DAD. FAST-FORWARD TO 16-YEAR-OLD SUGG IN SIXTH FORM AT CORSHAM SCHOOL BEING SET A MEDIA STUDIES ASSIGNMENT TO CREATE A TRAILER FOR AN APOCALYPTIC/DYSTOPIAN FILM. NOW, NORMALLY I WAS THE SORT OF KID IN SCHOOL WHO LEFT HIS HOMEWORK UNTIL THE LAST MINUTE. BUT THIS PROJECT WAS EXACTLY THE KIND OF THING I WAS INTERESTED IN AND FOR THE FIRST TIME IN MY LIFE NOT ONLY DID I DO THE HOMEWORK THE DAY IT WAS SET, I ACTUALLY DID EXTRA WORK IN MY SPARE TIME! AS IT HAPPENS, ONE OF MY MEDIA STUDIES TEACHERS LENT ME A WELL-KNOWN GRAPHIC NOVEL AND I WAS INSPIRED TO CREATE MY OWN GRAPHIC NOVEL TO ACCOMPANY THE TRAILER. SEE, STARTING TO MAKE SENSE, RIGHT?

AS MANY OF YOU WILL KNOW, AFTER I'D COMPLETED MY A-LEVELS I DECIDED TO DO AN APPRENTICESHIP AS A ROOF THATCHER WITH MY UNCLE GARY. I LOVED IT (EXCEPT FOR THE FROSTY MORNINGS) AND HAVE ALWAYS SAID IT'S GOOD TO KNOW I HAVE A FALL-BACK CAREER AND TRADE, BUT AT THE TIME I FELT I NEEDED TO FIND OTHER WAYS TO CHANNEL MY CREATIVITY. AROUND THE SAME TIME MY SISTER,

ZOE, HAD STARTED A YOUTUBE CHANNEL AND AFTER APPEARING IN A
COUPLE OF HER VIDEOS, I DECIDED YOUTUBE WOULD BE THE PLACE TO
PUT ALL THE CREATIVE STUFF I HAD INSIDE MY BRAIN.

THAT WAS BACK IN 2011 AND NOW — AS I SIT HERE WRITING THIS
INTRODUCTION — I LIVE IN LONDON, AND TRYING TO MAKE PEOPLE
LAUGH IN SHORT VIDEOS ON THE INTERNET IS MY FULL-TIME JOB —
AMAZING! BEFORE I KNEW IT MY AUDIENCE GREW AND GREW AND NOW
IT'S LARGER THAN I COULD HAVE EVER ANTICIPATED. THE SUCCESS
OF MY CHANNEL HAS GIVEN ME SO MANY AMAZING OPPORTUNITIES,
NOT LEAST ALLOWING ME TO CREATE MY OWN PIECE OF ART IN THE
FORM OF THIS GRAPHIC NOVEL. I HONESTLY REMEMBER HAVING A
MINI FLASHBACK AT THE START OF THIS PROCESS TO THE DAYS OF
READING *THE BEANO*, AND LATER SPENDING HOURS ON SOME DODGY
ILLUSTRATOR SOFTWARE TRYING TO CREATE A GRAPHIC NOVEL FRONT
COVER FOR AN A-LEVEL MEDIA STUDIES PROJECT.

BUT, MORE IMPORTANT THAN ALL THAT STUFF YOU'VE JUST READ, THE
BIGGEST INSPIRATION FOR THIS BOOK ARE THE AMAZING PEOPLE (YEP,
THAT'S YOU) THAT TAKE TIME OUT OF THEIR DAY NOT JUST TO SUPPORT
MY SILLY LITTLE VIDEOS, BUT TO SUPPORT ME IN EVERYTHING I DO. SO
MANY OF THE THINGS YOU'LL SEE AND READ IN THE FOLLOWING PAGES
ARE INSPIRED BY ISSUES THAT MY VIEWERS ARE HAVING, OR THINGS
YOU'RE GOING THROUGH AND HAVE SHARED WITH ME.

SO, FINALLY, I'D LIKE TO SAY ENJOY THE ADVENTURE THAT IS
USERNAME: EVIE, YOU'LL NEVER KNOW JUST HOW MUCH I APPRECIATE
WHAT YOU'VE DONE FOR ME AND THIS IS A LITTLE SOMETHING FROM ME
TO YOU — THIS ISN'T MY GRAPHIC NOVEL, IT'S OURS.

ALL THE BEST,

JOE

P.S. GUYS, UNDER NO CIRCUMSTANCES SHOULD YOU CLIMB INTO A
FRIDGE, JUMP OFF A ROOFTOP, OR DO ANY OF THE OTHER DANGEROUS
THINGS THAT EVIE DOES...

WHOEVER SAID "THERE'S AN APP FOR EVERYTHING" WAS SERIOUSLY MISTAKEN.

MRUUUUGHHH!

RIGHT NOW, I COULD TAKE A SELFIE THAT WOULD OWN THE INTERNET.

LIKE! LIKE! FOLLOW! FOLLOW! SUBSCRIBE!

I COULD SHARE IT TO GET ME LIKES AND FOLLOWERS.

BUT A SELFIE WON'T SAVE ME NOW.

I CAN'T EVEN GET A SIGNAL TO CALL FOR HELP.

I DIDN'T START THIS, OBVIOUSLY, BUT STOPPING IT IS DOWN TO ME.

WHOOOMP

I THINK WE ALL KNOW THE ODDS ARE AGAINST A HAPPY ENDING HERE.

♪WHEEEEWWWWHEEE♪

BUT THEN, I'M NOT EXACTLY ALONE.

I CAN DO THIS...

... WITH SOME HELP FROM A FRIEND...

... AND KNOWING THAT YOU'RE COMING WITH ME FOR THE RIDE...

SCREEE

6

PART ONE

MY DAD LIVED FOR HIS WORK AS A SOFTWARE PIONEER.

EVER SINCE I WAS A KID, HE'D ALWAYS BEEN CONSUMED BY SOME GRAND, CRAZY PROJECT.

I'LL BE WITH YOU IN A MOMENT, LOVE.

THEN HE GOT SICK AND I THOUGHT HE'D STOP...

... INSTEAD, HE RESPONDED LIKE A MAN ON BORROWED TIME.

WHATEVER YOU'RE WORKING ON CAN WAIT.

YOU NEED TO REST.

I'LL BE FINE.

HOW WAS YOUR DAY?

OH, NOTHING SPECIAL. THE USUAL.

THE USUAL?

"JUST HANGING OUT WITH FRIENDS..."

"... CATCHING UP ON GOSSIP..."

SHE LIVES IN A COTTAGE WITH A ROOF MADE FROM STRAW.

THAT MAKES HER A WITCH, RIGHT?

"... AND CHILLING WITH EVERYONE ON THE BUS."

EVIE, I'M WORRIED ABOUT YOU.

IF THERE'S ANYTHING I CAN DO...

I CAN TAKE CARE OF MYSELF, JUST AS I CAN TAKE CARE OF YOU.

DON'T LET THEM BEAT YOU, EVIE.

EVEN AFTER I'M GONE.

WHEN DAD GOT DIAGNOSED, I SOBBED MY EYES OUT FOR A NIGHT.

AFTER THAT, I DIDN'T SHED A SINGLE TEAR.

IN A WAY, FEELING SO NUMB MEANT NOTHING COULD MAKE THINGS WORSE.

EVEN BEING THE SCHOOL OUTCAST.

AT LEAST HERE I'M SAFE. AND FREE TO BE ME.

B-DING

Mallory

TODAY 16:19

TODAY 16:20

HUH?

SO, NOW THERE'S NO ESCAPE?

LET'S BE CLEAR HERE, WHEN TIMES GOT TOUGH I DIDN'T TURN TO COMFORT EATING.

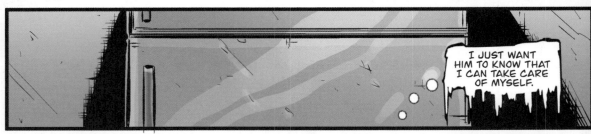

... SOMEWHERE WHERE I WON'T D-DIE FROM HYPOTHERMIA.

I WILL MAKE THIS HAPPEN...

CLACKETY TAP CLAK

... EVEN IF IT'S THE LAST THING THAT I DO.

CLACKETY TAP CLAK

KLIK
TAP
CLAK
TAP
TAP CLAK
KLIK
CLAK KLIK
TAP

LATER THAT WEEK...

MY PARENTS ARE OUT ON SATURDAY NIGHT. THEY WON'T EVEN KNOW!

I MEAN, WHY BOTHER ASKING WHEN THEY'D JUST REFUSE?

TRUST ME, THIS PARTY'S GONNA BE INSANE. EVERYONE'S COMING. APART FROM YOU-KNOW-WHO...

IT WOULD HURT LESS IF SHE WASN'T FAMILY.

AS COUSINS, IT'S FAIR TO SAY WE DIDN'T CLICK.

MALLORY:
PROM-QUEEN-IN-WAITING. ATTENTION MAGNET.

GIGGLE

GIGGLE

SNARF

EVEN AS KIDS, SHE HAD ISSUES WITH ME.

I GUESS SHE NEVER GREW OUT OF IT.

YOU'RE DOING THAT WRONG.

GIVE ME THAT!

NOW LOOK WHAT YOU'VE DONE!

POP

IT WAS AN ACCIDENT. I'M SORRY.

LEAVE MY TOYS ALONE!

AND GET OUT OF MY ROOM!

OH. ACTUALLY, I'M BUSY ON SATURDAY. I'VE BEEN INVITED TO THIS PARTY...

AH, I SEE.

ANOTHER TIME, MAYBE?

TAKE THEM ANYWAY. MAYBE WE CAN PLAY ON THE WAY HOME SOME TIME?

THANKS (I THINK).

BLANGALANG
BLANGALANG

I SHOULD GET GOING...

FRIDGE, YOU'VE BEEN GOOD TO ME WHEN TIMES ARE TOUGH, BUT THERE HAS TO BE A SAFER PLACE...

... I CAN'T FEEL MY TOES.

CLAK TAP TAP KLIK

DAD, I WAS THINKING. COULD WE HAVE A ROAST DINNER SOON?

EVER SINCE YOU WERE LITTLE, YOU'VE ASKED FOR THAT WHENEVER YOU NEED CHEERING UP...

DON'T LET THEM GET YOU DOWN, EVIE.

BE PROUD OF WHO YOU ARE, AND NEVER LOSE SIGHT OF THE FACT THAT YOU ARE LOVED.

HERE'S THE DEAL. I'LL SURVIVE, AND YOU COOK A ROAST CHICKEN WITH MY FAVOURITE YORKSHIRE PUDDINGS, OK?

I'LL MAKE THE BEST YOU EVER TASTED.

THANKS, DAD.

23:44 16%

Mallory

TODAY 23:43

TODAY 23:44

ARGHHH!

IT'S JUST ME.

IT WAS ALWAYS COMFORTING TO COME HOME TO THE SOUND OF TYPING...

... IT TOLD ME DAD WAS HERE.

SO THE SILENCE RANG ALARM BELLS.

DAD?

CREEEEE

NO.

NO!

DAD!!

MY PARENTS WERE SOULMATES.

THEY WERE MADE FOR EACH OTHER...

... THAT'S WHAT HE ALWAYS SAID...

... AND I COULD SEE IT IN EVERY PICTURE.

I DON'T REMEMBER MUCH ABOUT MUM. SHE DIED SO LONG AGO.

BUT DAD KEPT HER MEMORY ALIVE WITH STORIES ABOUT OUR TIME TOGETHER.

NOW IT FELL TO ME TO MAKE SURE THAT DAD WOULD NEVER BE FORGOTTEN.

HE HAD GONE, BUT I WOULD CARRY HIM IN MY HEART...

... WHATEVER LIFE HAD IN STORE FOR ME.

WE GATHER HERE TO COMMEND OUR BROTHER AND LOVING FATHER...

SOB SNIFFLE

AT A TIME OF LOSS, EVERYTHING SEEMS TO HAPPEN BEFORE YOU'RE READY.

IT FEELS LIKE THE PEOPLE AROUND YOU KNOW HOW TO MOVE ON...

... WHILE THINGS HAVE TO CHANGE BECAUSE IT'S "FOR THE BEST"...

FOR SALE

IT COULD'VE BEEN WORSE, I GUESS.

KNOCK KNOCK

AT LEAST COUSIN MALLORY SHOWED SHE HAD A HEART.

EVIE, THINGS HAVE NEVER BEEN GREAT BETWEEN US, BUT IF THERE'S ANYTHING I CAN DO...

...JUST SAY THE WORD AND I'LL DROP EVERYTHING.

BRRNNGG

I NEED TO GET THIS.

BRRNNGG

JASPAR! THAT SHOT OF YOU ON THE ROOF IS EVERYWHERE!

OK, SO MAYBE SHE DIDN'T HAVE A HUMAN HEART, BUT IT WAS A START.

EVEN THE FRIDGE WAS OUT OF BOUNDS.

IT'S GREAT TO SEE YOU SETTLING IN WITH US.

MALLORY IS SO PLEASED YOU'RE HERE.

ISN'T THAT *RIGHT*, HONEY?

IT'S A THRILL. WHEN IS TEA?

I'LL CALL YOU WHEN IT'S READY.

I SHOULD GET OUT OF YOUR WAY.

RIGHT NOW...

... ALL I WANT TO DO...

... IS DISAPPEAR.

IF ONLY YOU COULD'VE KNOWN HOW COMFORTING THIS SOUNDS.

TAP
CLAK
TAP

BEEDOOP

WHOA!

HMMM...

E.SCAPE

KNOCK KNOCK

YOU LOOK LIKE YOU'VE SEEN A GHOST.

BEEP BEELOOP BEEP

CAN I TALK TO YOU?

I FEEL LIKE I MIGHT BREAK IF I DON'T OPEN UP TO SOMEONE.

I SUPPOSE.

BEEP   BEEP

I KNOW THIS ISN'T EASY FOR EITHER OF US, BUT I JUST FEEL SO...

... SO LONELY.

BEELOOP

MALLORY?

IT DOESN'T MATTER.

23:44   26%

Jaspar

TODAY 23:42

U R sooo cute

Tell me a secret...

Wot kind?

Use ur imagination

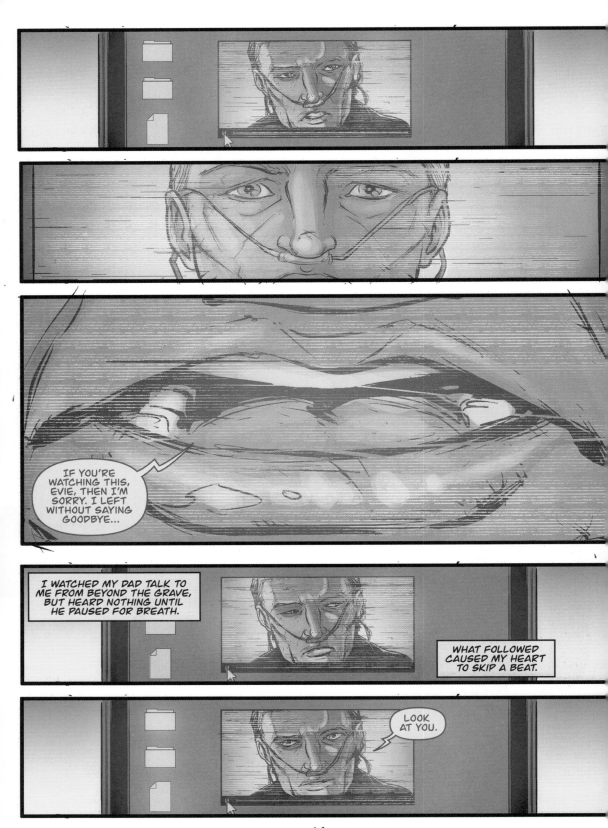

47

48

PART TWO

IT HAD BEEN A LONG WHILE SINCE I WALKED LIKE THIS...

... WITH MY HEAD UP HIGH.

WHENEVER I ENCOUNTERED PEOPLE, I JUST SMILED...

... AND THEY SMILED RIGHT BACK AT ME.

MY CONFIDENCE GREW WITH EVERY STEP...

... AS DID MY WONDER FOR THIS WORLD.

HMM...

FOR ONCE IN YOUR LIFE, EVIE, YOU DON'T NEED TO AVOID ANYONE.

JUST GO WITH THE FLOW.

WHO KNEW IT WOULD FEEL *THIS* GOOD?

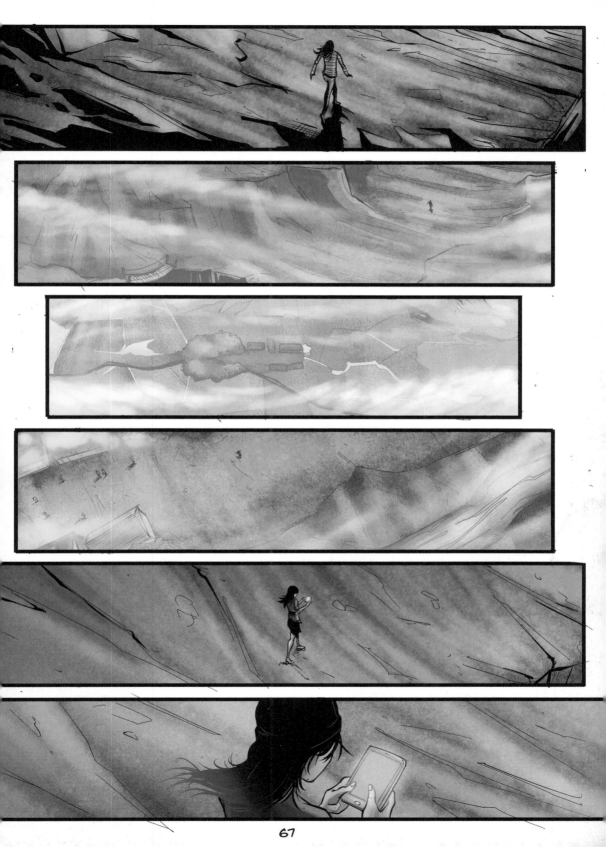

TO WELCOME AND CONSOLE. THAT IS MY FUNCTION.

BUT FROM HERE I CAN ALSO OBSERVE.

AN OVERSIGHT, PERHAPS, IN THE CREATOR'S MASTER PLAN.

YOU'RE MISTAKING ME FOR SOMEONE.

BUT YOU LOOK JUST LIKE HIM!

EVEN BETTER, IN FACT...

EVIE, I'M JUST A LINE OF CODE IN A GRAND PROGRAM.

IF I LOOK AND SOUND FAMILIAR, IT'S BECAUSE YOU WERE THINKING OF THAT PERSON WHEN YOU BUMPED INTO ME.

LET'S HOPE I LIVE UP TO YOUR EXPECTATIONS, EH?

I DIDN'T CARE THAT HE WAS A DIGITAL JASPAR. HE KNEW MY NAME.

MAYBE I CAN WALK WITH YOU? I'LL PROTECT YOU FROM THE PIGEONS.

LET'S GO!

IF PARADISE HAD A CAPITAL CITY, I WAS AT THE HEART OF IT.

THIS IS SO NICE.

IF YOU'RE HAPPY, THEN SO AM I.

JUST THEN, I DIDN'T THINK I'D EVER WANT TO LEAVE.

THIS BEATS BOATING ANY DAY.

COUNT ME IN FOR SOME CHAOS!

EASY THERE, BUDDY!

IF YOU'RE GOING TO RUN WILD...

... AT LEAST LET ME SHOW YOU HOW IT'S DONE!

C'MON, LET'S DO THIS!!

GRAAHH

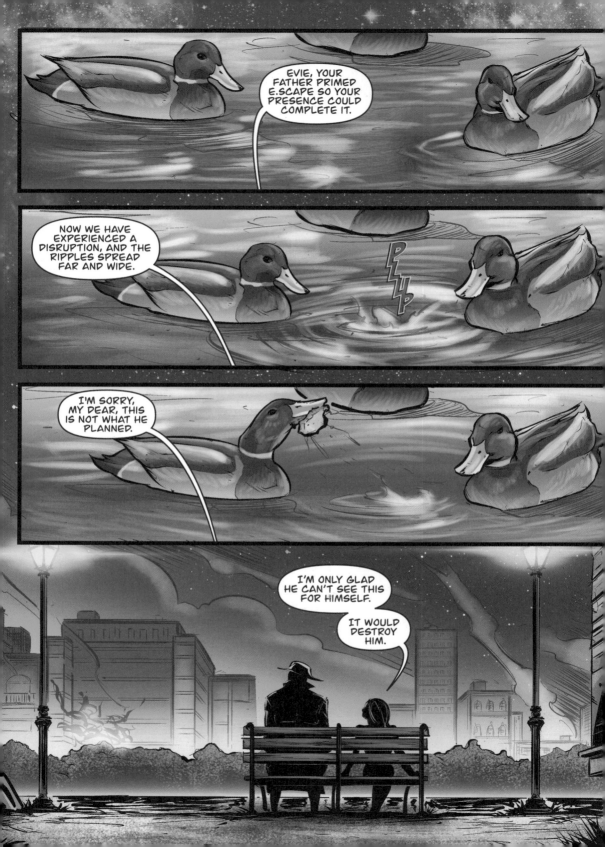

PLUP

THERE IS ONE WAY TO SAVE E.SCAPE.

WHAT DO YOU HAVE IN MIND?

AN ARMY OR A MIRACLE?

NEITHER...

JUST SEEK OUT THE CREATOR...

... AND TELL HIM FOR YOURSELF.

BUT DAD IS GONE.

HE *DIED.*

IN THE *PHYSICAL* SENSE, YES...

... DIGITALLY... *ANYTHING* IS POSSIBLE.

YOUR FATHER WIRED UP THIS WORLD.

I GUESS HE WAS ENTITLED TO CODE HIMSELF INTO IT.

THE QUESTION IS WHERE.

AND WHETHER YOU CAN TRACK HIM DOWN BEFORE IT'S TOO LATE.

WHERE DO I BEGIN?

YOU KNOW HIM BETTER THAN ANYONE, EVIE.

BACK HOME IT FELT LIKE WE LIVED ON THE EDGE OF CIVILISATION. DAD SAID THAT'S WHERE IT SUITED HIM...

... HE NEEDED SPACE TO THINK...

... HE'S AS FAR FROM HERE AS I COULD POSSIBLY IMAGINE, ISN'T HE?

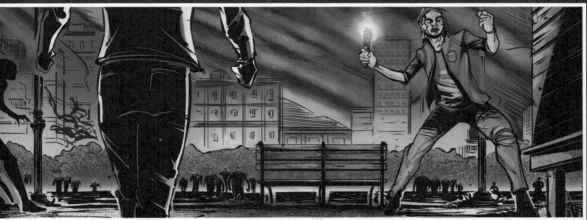

WHAT JUST HAPPENED?

DID I HURT IT?

WHAT'S TURNING THEM INTO SUCH MONSTERS?

SOMETHING BAD, EVIE. A DISRUPTIVE INFLUENCE...

ONE THING IS FOR SURE, THINGS ARE GROWING DARKER THAN I FEARED.

OK, SO NOW I'M REALLY FREAKING OUT...

... AND ONLY YOU CAN STOP IT FROM SPREADING.

SO, I HAD NO MAP TO FIND MY DAD. NO WAY OF KNOWING WHAT DIRECTION TO HEAD.

ALL I COULD DO WAS FOLLOW MY INSTINCTS.

HEAD AS FAR AS MY FEET WOULD TAKE ME, AND HOPE FOR THE BEST.

DON'T JOIN THEM...

≈GASP≈

PLEASE! IT'S SO SENSELESS.

MY HEAD TOLD ME TO FLEE. MY HEART STOPPED ME IN MY TRACKS.

THERE WAS JUST SOMETHING ABOUT THIS SORRY FIGURE I COULDN'T IGNORE.

AND I SENSED HE FELT THE SAME ABOUT ME.

I'M NOT LIKE THEM.

LIKEWISE... I CAN'T EXACTLY HIDE IT.

DON'T STARE AT ME.

IT'S OK...

IT SEEMS WE BOTH FACE STRUGGLES.

HE DIDN'T SPEAK MUCH.

I DIDN'T EVEN KNOW HIS NAME.

BUT WITHIN A FEW BLOCKS IT FELT LIKE I'D KNOWN HIM FOREVER.

I NO LONGER FELT ALONE.

WE WERE IN THIS TOGETHER...

... AND THAT'S HOW WE WOULD FIND MY FATHER.

IF YOU'LL ALLOW ME TO STEAL THE SPOTLIGHT FOR A MOMENT...

... AND CAN I SAY HOW *HOT* YOU LOOK, ALL FIRED UP.

MRRHHHH?

LISTEN UP, PEOPLE.

LET'S MAKE SOME NOISE FOR OUR QUEEN OF MISRULE.

THE OTHER VISITOR WOULD NEVER DREAM OF TAKING THINGS THIS FAR.

NOW MAKE SOME *NOISE!*

HRUGGHH!

HRUGGHH!

MRAUW

WHERE DO I FIND HER?

SEARCH ME.

LET ME GIVE YOU ONE MORE CHANCE TO ANSWER.

YANK

WHERE...

IS SHE??

I'LL PUT THE WORD OUT ON THE STREET...

... IF YOU'LL LET ME PEEL MY FACE OFF IT FIRST.

IF MY JOURNEY INTO THE CITY WAS A DREAM, THE ROUTE OUT WAS A NIGHTMARE. ONE THAT GREW DARKER BY THE MILE.

MURHH

IT WAS AS IF A VIRUS HAD SPREAD ACROSS THIS LAND.

GRRK

POISONING THE POPULATION.

BLACKENING THEIR HEARTS.

AND TURNING THEM AGAINST US.

GRAWW

IT FORCED US TO MOVE LIKE GHOSTS.

UNDER COVER OF DARKNESS...

... AND DRAW STRENGTH FROM EACH OTHER TO KEEP PUSHING ON.

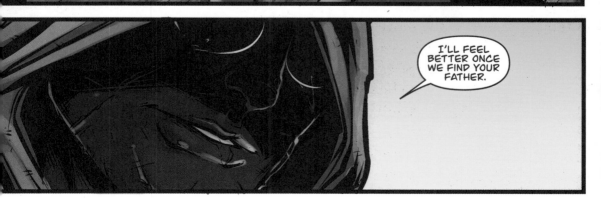

TOGETHER, WE MADE SANDWICHES.

THEY WERE THE BEST I'D EVER TASTED.

MAYBE WE SHOULD STAY HERE OVERNIGHT.

I'M NOT SO SURE, EVIE.

BUT NOTHING CAN HARM US IN HERE. WE'LL JUST PUT ANOTHER LOG ON THE BURNER AND CURL UP LIKE THAT CAT.

HEY KITTY, KITTY...

OMIGOD!!! WHAT IS THAT?

SHHH!!

SKrEEEE

HSSSSSSS

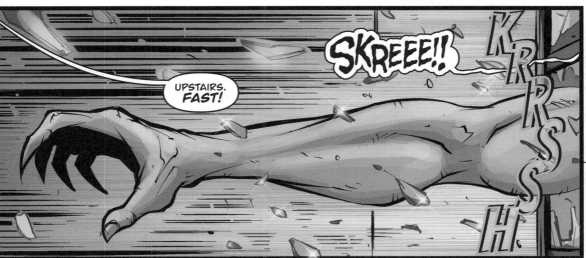

E.SCAPE WAS INTENDED AS A SAFE PLACE.

INSTEAD, IT'S BECOME A CAULDRON OF FEAR AND UNREST.

AND ALL AT THE HANDS OF ONE PERSON.

A TROUBLED INDIVIDUAL HELL-BENT ON MAKING EVIE FEEL SMALL, SO SHE FEELS BIG.

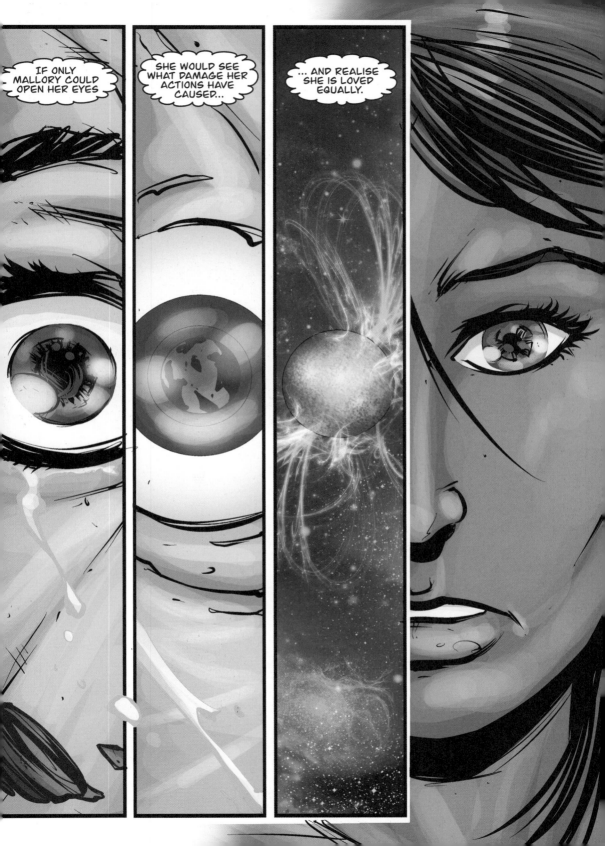

PART THREE

IT'S GETTING REALLY DARK.

IF WE STOP NOW, WE MAY NEVER SEE THE LIGHT OF DAY AGAIN!

HAVING COME THIS FAR, I DIDN'T KNOW WHAT TO EXPECT.

A PALACE, MAYBE.

SOME PLACE FITTING FOR THE PERSON WHO CREATED THIS WORLD FROM CODE.

AND THEN I REMINDED MYSELF JUST WHO WE WERE SEARCHING FOR.

DAD!

BACK HOME I USED TO FINISH READING AND FIND YOU'D LEFT ME A NICE CUP OF TEA.

IT WAS ALWAYS STONE-COLD BY THEN, OF COURSE.

DAD, I'M AFRAID A COLD CUP OF TEA IS THE LEAST OF OUR WORRIES NOW.

THIS PLACE YOU CREATED JUST FOR ME, A SAFE PLACE... WELL, IT ISN'T SO SAFE ANYMORE.

HOW CAN THAT BE? YOU'RE A GOOD SOUL.

E.SCAPE CAN ONLY THRIVE ON YOUR INFLUENCE.

WE'RE NOT TALKING ABOUT MY INFLUENCE.

SOMEONE ELSE IS HERE?

AND JUST LOOK AT THE CONSEQUENCES.

THE CHERRY TREE ISN'T JUST YOUR GATEWAY INTO E.SCAPE.

I DESIGNED IT TO REFLECT YOUR IMPACT ON THE WORLD AROUND YOU.

A FORCE FOR GOOD WILL SEE THE TREE FLOURISH.

A BAD INFLUENCE...

LET'S JUST SAY THAT UNITY ISN'T ALONE IN HOPING THAT THE BLOSSOM SURVIVES THIS ONSLAUGHT.

YOU DON'T SOUND TOO CONFIDENT, SIR.

WE WOULDN'T JUST LOSE A THING OF BEAUTY.

DAD, TALK TO US!

WHAT HAPPENS IF THE TREE LOSES ITS BLOSSOM?

THEN... THEN E.SCAPE WILL BE CORRUPTED BEYOND REPAIR.

WE NEED TO LEAVE, EVIE. AND *FAST!*

THAT BLOSSOM WON'T HOLD ON FOR LONG.

BUT I NEVER EVEN THOUGHT I'D *SEE* YOU AGAIN. CAN'T WE STAY HERE TOGETHER?

I'VE ALREADY LOST YOU ONCE.

EVIE, YOU'RE HERE TO RECHARGE SO YOU CAN FACE THE WORLD FEELING STRONGER.

HIDING FROM IT WON'T SOLVE ANYTHING. AS MUCH AS IT BREAKS MY HEART TO SAY THIS, YOU HAVE TO GO... NOW.

IN A PERFECT WORLD, I'D INVITE YOU TO STAY FOR SOMETHING TO EAT.

WE COULD'VE HAD THAT ROAST I PROMISED.

EXTRA YORKSHIRE PUDDINGS, TOO.

NOW THAT WOULD MAKE *EVERYTHING* BETTER!

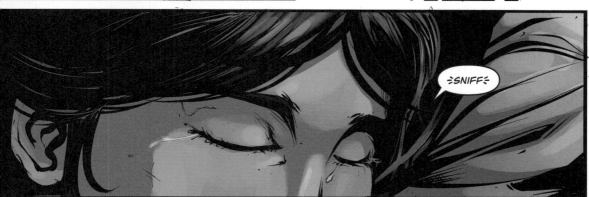

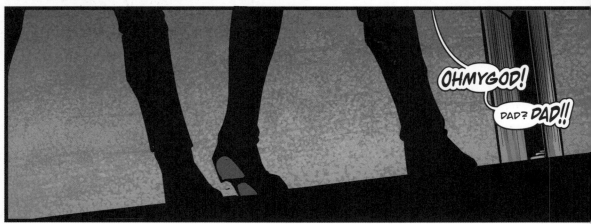

ENOUGH! STOP!

IT'S OVER.

WOW! LOOKS LIKE EVIE CALLED THE SHOTS HERE ALL ALONG.

SHE ALWAYS DID.

ALWAYS WILL.

WHAT JUST HAPPENED?

I FEEL LIKE I'VE WOKEN FROM A BAD DREAM!

DO WE STILL HAVE TIME TO REACH THE TREE?

THERE'S NO GUARANTEE YOU'LL MAKE IT NOW.

I'LL GIVE IT MY BEST SHOT, SIR. YOU CAN COUNT ON ME!

WAIT A SECOND...

WITH EVERY STEP THIS WORLD CONTINUED TO TURN AGAINST US.

A WILD WIND HOWLED ACROSS THE LAND.

RAIN LASHED OUR FACES.

LIGHTNING SPAT FROM THE SKY.

WHILE THE POPULATION RAMPAGED AGAINST ITSELF — A SPARK THAT HAD IGNITED A FIREBALL.

"... AND EVER AFTER."

NEXT MORNING

HAHA! NO WAY? REALLY!

UPLOAD THAT!

MIND IF I JOIN YOU?

LIONEL!

THAT'S MY NAME. DON'T WIRE IT UP.

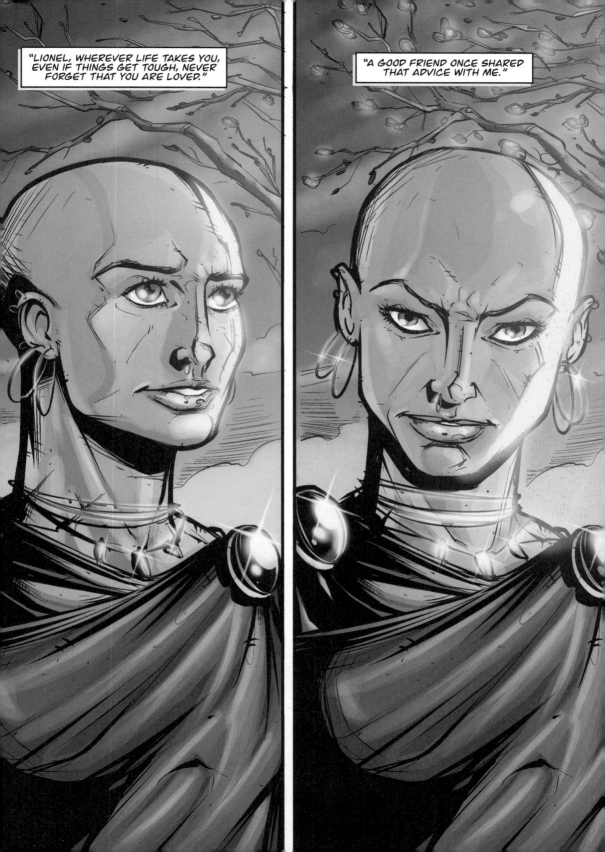

THANK YOUs

FIRST AND FOREMOST I'D LIKE TO THANK **YOU** FOR READING THIS RIGHT NOW, AND FOR YOUR AMAZING SUPPORT. IT MEANS THE WORLD TO ME THAT YOU LOVE WHAT I DO SO MUCH :)

ALSO BIG UP BRIONY, LENI AND THE REST OF HODDER FOR BEING THE BEST/MOST PATIENT PUBLISHER CREW I COULD ASK FOR. ENORMOUS THANKS TO THE REST OF THE SUGG SQUAD, MATT WHYMAN & AMRIT BIRDI. TOGETHER, WE HAVE CREATED SOMETHING VERY SPECIAL TO ME.

A MASSIVE THANK YOU TO LUCY LENDREM, ALEX CLARKE AND DOM SMALES AT GLEAM FOR PUTTING UP WITH ME. SHOUT OUT TO MY YOUTUBE BUDDIES — YOU KNOW WHO YOU ALL ARE! THANKS TO CASPAR LEE & OLI WHITE FOR JUST BEING GENERAL LEGENDS AND NOT HURTING ME AFTER I CONSTANTLY PRANK AND WIND THEM UP.

THANKS TO ALL MY FRIENDS BACK HOME IN WILTSHIRE FOR THE SUPPORT AND REMINDING ME THAT I MAY BE DOING ALL THIS COOL STUFF, BUT I'M STILL USELESS AT DOWNING A PINT.

THANKS TO BOTH MY NANS AND GRANDDAD, MY MUM AND DAD, AND OF COURSE, LAST BUT NOT LEAST...

THANKS TO MY BIG SIS, ZOE. YOU FILMED AND EDITED MY FIRST TWO VIDEOS, GAVE ME ALL YOUR HAND-ME-DOWN LAPTOPS AND FILMING EQUIPMENT TO HELP ME START MY YOUTUBE CHANNEL, AND HAVE GIVEN ME SOME OF THE BEST SISTERLY ADVICE ONLINE AND OFFLINE. BUT, ABOVE ALL THAT, YOU'RE JUST A PRETTY GREAT SISTER. WELL DONE, MATE.